DEAR STUDENT,
MAGIC POTIONS AND ELIXIRS IS A TEXTBOOK
I WROTE FOR THE COURSE I TEACH AT THE
NORTH LANDING ACADEMY OF MAGIC ARTS.

I ALWAYS START THIS COURSE BY TELLING MY STUDENTS
THESE THREE FACTS:

1.

POTIONS ARE LIQUID SPELLS.

FOLLOW THE RULES OF SPELL CASTING TO MAKE YOUR POTIONS.

2.

THE WORD **POTION** COMES FROM
THE LATIN WORD POTIO, WHICH MEANS A DRINK.
BUT MOST TRUE POTIONS ARE NOT DRINKS.

3.

THE MOST DIFFICULT PART OF POTION MAKING
IS FINDING AND PREPARING THE RIGHT **INGREDIENTS**.
INGREDIENTS ARE SUBSTANCES YOU USE
TO MAKE A MAGIC POTION, OR TO COOK A MEAL.

What Makes Magic

My friends know that I am a professor at a magic school, and often invite me to their kids' parties where they mix dish soap with glitter and call that a magic potion. Splish-splash, lots of foam and bubbles, kids are happy... soap and glitter are all over the place. Fun!

But you and I know that splashing around and making a mess is not magic.

Magic is sending your will out there like a ray of light, to change something in the world. So it's all about your intention. It's more important what you think, than what you mix. That's why we **prepare** our magic ingredients so carefully, we **clean** our work space, and make our potions **beautiful**. Your intention to make magic must be strong, and that means **putting effort into your work**. The more effort, the better your result.

Take time to prepare. Learn to **take care of every detail**. Focus. And one day you will be able to mix dish soap with glitter and turn it into a real potion, because

IT'S YOUR MIND THAT MAKES MAGIC,
not the bubbles. Get it?

Potion

A MAGIC POTION IS AN **ENCHANTED INFUSION** USED IN SPELLS.
WHAT IS AN INFUSION?
INFUSION IS WHEN YOU LEAVE THINGS
LIKE PLANTS OR ROCKS IN WATER
OR OIL FOR SOME HOURS OR DAYS,
SO THAT THE WATER OR OIL
RECEIVES THEIR ENERGY.
ENCHANTED MEANS UNDER A MAGIC SPELL.
IF YOU PUT A SPELL ON TAP WATER, IT'S ENCHANTED WATER.

MOST PEOPLE THINK A MAGIC POTION IS A DRINK. NO!
YOU SPRINKLE YOUR POTION ON THINGS OR PEOPLE,
YOU USE IT TO WASH YOUR HANDS OR CLOTHES,
YOU CAN ADD IT TO A BATH, BUT . . .
THE IDEA OF DRINKING A POTION PROBABLY
CAME FROM THE STORIES ABOUT *LOVE POTIONS*.
SEE THE CHAPTER *ARE LOVE POTIONS REAL?*

DON'T DRINK IT

Elixir

AN ELIXIR IS A MAGIC LIQUID USED TO MAKE A PERSON FEEL
BETTER. IF YOU ARE SAD OR TIRED, AN ELIXIR CAN HELP.
ELIXIRS ARE ALSO USED FOR HEALING WOUNDS OR TREATING
DISEASES, BUT YOU HAVE TO BE
A REAL MAGIC DOCTOR
TO MAKE AN ELIXIR LIKE THAT.
ELIXIRS ARE NOT INFUSED
LIKE POTIONS, THEY ARE MIXED
FROM DIFFERENT INGREDIENTS,
AND CAN BE USED RIGHT AWAY.

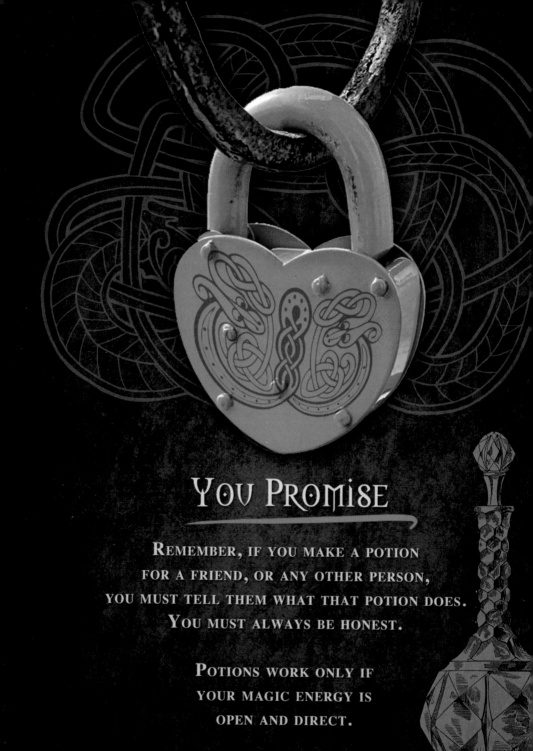

You Promise

REMEMBER, IF YOU MAKE A POTION
FOR A FRIEND, OR ANY OTHER PERSON,
YOU MUST TELL THEM WHAT THAT POTION DOES.
YOU MUST ALWAYS BE HONEST.

POTIONS WORK ONLY IF
YOUR MAGIC ENERGY IS
OPEN AND DIRECT.

"A WORD TO THE WISE IS SUFFICIENT"
("SAPIENTI SAT" IN LATIN, *SAH-PEA-EN-TEA SAHT*)

The Moon Potion

This potion is said to bring you a victory over an enemy.

It comes from the time of the Vikings. We know this because to make this potion you need to cut the shape of the **T** or **Tyr** rune from a green leaf. This rune was a letter of the Viking alphabet, and a magic **symbol of victory.** You will need:

- A glass of milk
- A slice of bread
- A green leaf and scissors

Tyr has the shape of an arrow pointing up. Cut it out of a green leaf like this. Drink a sip of milk, then drop Tyr into into the milk, saying:

Moon, drink of my cup, then fill it up. **Earth,** give me a sign that Victory is mine.

Pour the milk outside, drawing a circle on the ground, put the bread in the middle of the circle, and leave it for the birds.

Did you know that Tyr is the **Tue** in the word **Tuesday?** The English names of the days of the week come from ancient Northern Europe and use names of planets and gods (Tyr, Odin, Thor, Freya).

**Sunday - Sun's Day • Monday - Moon's Day
Tuesday - Tyr's (or Tiw's) Day • Wednesday - Odin's Day
Thursday - Thor's Day • Friday - Freya's Day (Venus)
Saturday - Saturn's Day**

The Seven Birds Elixir

A healing potion

THIS ELIXIR HELPS HEAL A WOUND, OR A COLD. REMEMBER, YOU DON'T DRINK TRUE ELIXIRS! ONCE YOUR *SEVEN BIRDS* ELIXIR IS READY, DIP YOUR FINGER IN IT AND USE IT TO DRAW A CIRCLE AROUND THE WOUND, OR DRAW A CIRCLE ON THE BACK OF YOUR RIGHT HAND TO HEAL A HEADACHE, COLD, OR FLU.

THIS ELIXIR IS MADE FROM PLANT ROOTS. THE LIFE ENERGY OF A PLANT IS IN ITS ROOTS, THAT'S WHY ROOTS ARE OFTEN USED IN POTION MAKING.

EVEN IF IT'S WINTER, YOU CAN DIG UP SOME PLANT ROOTS. IF IT'S SUMMER, LOOK FOR DANDELIONS OR CHICORY. THEY GROW EVERYWHERE, AND THEIR ROOTS ARE GREAT FOR POTIONS. WASH 7 PIECES OF ROOTS, PUT THEM IN A JAR OR A BOTLE OF WATER, AND SAY:

7 BIRDS FLY FROM EAST TO WEST
7 ROOTS THEY BRING TO THEIR NEST
7 BIRDS, ARE THESE ROOTS FOR A MAGIC SPELL?
YES, THESE ROOTS ARE FOR YOU. THEY WILL MAKE YOU WELL.
SEAL THE JAR AND PUT IT IN A DARK PLACE FOR 3 HOURS.
WHEN YOU OPEN THE JAR, SAY:
ON COUNT 3 MY WORD IS THE KEY.
COUNT TO 3 AND OPEN THE JAR.

THIS IS ME COLLECTING ROCKS
FOR MY POTIONS CLASS AT
THE NORTH LANDING ACADEMY OF MAGIC ARTS.
BELIEVE ME, I KNEW THAT DRAGON
WAS BEHIND ME WHEN THIS PICTURE WAS TAKEN.
AFTER YEARS AT NORTH LANDING, YOU FEEL THEM COMING.
A HORIZON CIRCLE WITH MY WAND TOOK CARE OF THAT ONE.

The New Beginning (1)

THIS POTION HELPS A NEW PROJECT TO BE A SUCCESS

You will need:
- An egg (hard-boiled)
- A tall glass of water
- A pen or marker
- 4 small rocks, 4 leaves
- flowers or grass

This potion is a bit tricky. We need to write a spell on the egg, then drop it into the potion. Raw eggs can easily break, so use a hard-boiled egg.
The spell to write on the egg is:
Ab Initio Mundi
(which means "from the beginning of the world" in Latin)
The egg has always been a symbol of life and new beginning. For example, in Ancient Egypt, they believed the world came from an egg. We give eggs as gifts for Easter. In this spell we call on the magic force present in the world since its beginning.

Now the tricky part. You need to put the egg into a glass of water in a way that
1. THE GLASS IS FULL
2. NO WATER SPILLS FROM THE GLASS.

If your glass is full, and you put an egg in it, some water will spill (Why? See the next page). We need to measure the water before you start your potion-making ritual.

ARCHIMEDES
WHY WATER SPILLS...

ARCHIMEDES WAS AN ANCIENT GREEK
MATHEMATICIAN. ONE DAY HE GOT
IN A BATH TUB THAT WAS FULL.
SOME WATER SPILLED. ARCHIMEDES
GUESSED THAT IT SPILLS BECAUSE HIS
BODY TAKES THE SPACE, AND PUSHES
THE WATER OUT. THE BODY GOES IN,
THE WATER GOES OUT. THERE IS NOT
ENOUGH ROOM FOR BOTH! HE WAS
SO EXCITED, HE SCREAMED "EUREKA!"
(WHICH MEANS "I FOUND IT!"

IN GREEK). LATER HE DISCOVERED THAT THE AMOUNT OF WATER
THAT SPILLS IS AS BIG AS THE BODY THAT PUSHES THE WATER OUT.

SO HERE IS WHAT TO DO. 1. PUT YOUR EGG INTO
AN EMPTY GLASS, THEN FILL IT WITH WATER.
2. NEXT, HOLDING THE EGG, POUR ALL THE WATER
OUT INTO ANOTHER GLASS. 3. REFILL THE FIRST
GLASS WITH THE WATER FROM THE SECOND GLASS.
NOW THE WATER WON'T SPILL WHEN YOU PUT AN EGG
INTO IT, AND THE GLASS WILL BE FULL.

1.

2.

hold
the egg

3.

The New Beginning (2)

Now that you have measured
the amount of water you need
for the potion, focus on your
new project, and put the egg
into the glass with these words:

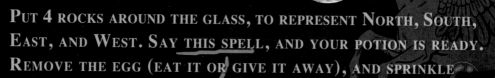

I plant this seed without fear.
Grow up and up from here.

Put 4 rocks around the glass, to represent North, South,
East, and West. Say this spell, and your potion is ready.
Remove the egg (eat it or give it away), and sprinkle
the potion inside and outside
the door to your house.

In the East
Is the morning light.
It is a promise -
Clear and bright.
In the North
Is the Polar Star.
It shows the way
Wherever you are.
The West brings together
The sun and the sea.
It gives me strength
It makes me free.
In the South
The Moon comes out.
I cast away
Any fear or doubt.

Liquid Shield

Is there an animal making a mess in your yard, or a person you dislike? Keep them away with this potion!

Some rocks you find outside glitter under the sun. Most rocks are made of many minerals (substances that make rocks) that melted and mixed in the hot layers under the crust of the Earth, or in a volcano. If you find a sparkly rock, it will probably have one of these minerals:

Quartz or Mica.

Bits of mica in a rock look like flat pieces of glitter, but grains of quartz are usually uneven or rounded.

The amazing thing about these sparkly rocks is that at night they collect the magic energy of moonlight. They share it when you use them in potions.

1. To clean your rock of any wrong energy, keep it in a bowl of warm water with salt for a few minutes.

2. Put it into a glass of water.

3. Holding the glass in one hand, and your magic wand in the other, say this spell:

Moonlight Dragon, guard my door.
[Say the name of the *unwelcome guest*]
Come no more.

4. With the glass and the wand in your hands, slowly walk around, first in a circle, and then following the shape of the infinity sign. → ∞

If you spill the water, you have to start it all over again!

5. Sprinkle the potion in front of your door.

BEFORE GLASS

MICA, ONE OF THE MINERALS IN THE SHINY ROCKS YOU
FIND OUTSIDE, PEELS OFF SOME STONES IN
THIN SLICES LIKE THIS.
THAT'S WHY, IN THE MIDDLE AGES,
WHEN GLASS WAS RARE AND EXPENSIVE,
THEY USED MICA TO MAKE WINDOWS!
GEOLOGY (*SCIENCE ABOUT THE EARTH AND THE MATERIALS IT'S
MADE FROM*) CALLS THESE MICA STONES MUSCOVITE, BECAUSE
IN THE MIDDLE AGES THEY CAME FROM MOSCOW, RUSSIA,
WHERE MANY HOUSES HAD MUSCOVITE WINDOWS LIKE THIS.

IN EUROPE IN THE MIDDLE AGES THEY ALSO
MADE WINDOWS FROM COW HORNS.
THE HORNS WERE KEPT IN WATER FOR
3 MONTHS UNTIL SOFT, THEN PRESSED
FLAT. THOSE WINDOWS LET IN
VERY LITTLE LIGHT. THEY ALSO
USED ANIMAL SKINS IN WINDOWS.

THE WORD WINDOW COMES FROM
2 ANCIENT WORDS: WIND + EYE.
THE MOST ANCIENT WINDOWS
WERE JUST OPENINGS IN THE WALLS
WITH THE WIND BLOWING FREELY
THROUGH THEM.

SO WHERE WERE THE FIRST GLASS WINDOWS MADE?
IN ANCIENT ROME, AROUND 100 A.D.
WHAT IS GLASS MADE FROM? GLASS IS MADE FROM SAND
BY HEATING IT UP UNTIL IT MELTS AND BECOMES GLASS.

Rain Erase

Do you want someone to forget something?
Have you said or done anything that is better forgotten?

That's what Rain Erase potion does. You will need to collect some real rain water to make this potion. You also need

- a bottle with a cork
- pen and paper, thread or ribbon
- leaves, grass, flowers, or twigs
- salt

Think of 3-5 words that describe what should be forgotten. For example: *I made a bad mistake.* Write it on a small piece of paper, roll it up, tie it and put it in a bottle together with some leaves or flowers. Add salt, fill the bottle with rain water, seal it, and shake it. Say:

What's written will my rain erase
Without a sign, without a trace.
Like darkness leaves before the dawn
Let this memory be gone.

Pour out the water,
and bury the paper
and leaves
in the ground outside.

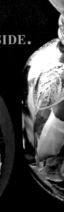

SALT IS OFTEN USED IN POTIONS. WHY?

SALT CAN PRESERVE FOOD: IT KILLS BACTERIA.
THAT'S WHY THEY PUT SALT IN PICKLES.
IN MAGIC ARTS SALT IS USED IN PROTECTION SPELLS
AND ALSO TO DESTROY HARMFUL OR EVIL FORCES.
SALT COMES EITHER FROM THE
OCEAN, OR FROM SALT MINES.
IF YOU LET OCEAN WATER DRY UP,
YOU'LL GET SALT. SALT MINES ARE
PLACES THAT WERE UNDER
THE OCEAN IN ANCIENT TIMES.
WHEN THE WATER DRIED UP,
IT LEFT A LOT OF SALT BEHIND.

WHAT DO **SALAD** AND **SALARY** HAVE IN COMMON?
THE WORD SALAD COMES FROM LATIN SAL (SALT)
ANCIENT ROMANS STARTED ADDING SALT TO THEIR VEGETABLES
AND INVENTED SALAD! SALARY (MONEY YOU ARE PAID
ON THE JOB) COMES FROM LATIN SALARIUM - MONEY
ROMAN SOLDIERS RECEIVED TO BUY SALT.

IN *ALCHEMY* (WHICH WAS A MIX
OF CHEMISTRY AND MAGIC)
SALT WAS A SYMBOL OF KNOWLEDGE.

*THIS IS ALCHEMICAL
SYMBOL FOR SALT*

SALT CAN DISSOLVE IN WATER AND
BECOME INVISIBLE, BUT WHEN SEA WATER
DRIES, PURE SALT CRYSTALS REMAIN. AND SO IT IS THAT
OUR KNOWLEDGE OF THE WORLD COMES FROM THINGS
VISIBLE AND INVISIBLE, AND GROWS CRYSTAL-CLEAR.

FLOWER POWDER

THIS IS A SECRET INGREDIENT IN MANY POWERFUL POTIONS.

IT TAKES TIME TO PREPARE YOUR POTION INGREDIENTS. SOMETIMES YOU HAVE TO START WORKING ON THEM DAYS OR MONTHS IN ADVANCE. SOME POTIONS USE DRY FLOWERS. WHETHER YOU PLUCK A FLOWER OUTSIDE OR BUY IT, YOU NEED 2-3 WEEKS TO DRY IT. IT HAS TO BE VERY DRY, SO YOU CAN CRUSH IT INTO POWDER.

CUT LEAVES OFF THE FLOWER, AND HANG IT HEAD DOWN IN A DRY DARK PLACE, LIKE A CLOSET OR A GARAGE. YOU CAN ALSO DRY FLOWERS LYING IN AN OPEN BOX, BUT IF YOU HANG THEM, THEY WILL HAVE THE SAME SHAPE AS WHEN THEY WERE FRESH. THEN THEY CAN SIT IN A VASE UNTIL IT'S TIME TO USE THEM IN A POTION.

CRUSH DRIED FLOWERS INTO POWDER WITH MORTAR AND PESTLE, OR WITH A FORK, AND STORE IT IN SEALED JARS. PINK-RED POWDER MIXED WITH WATER AND SPRINKLED ON YOUR FOREHEAD GIVES YOU POWER TO SEE THE TRUTH AND LEARN SECRETS. YELLOW-WHITE POWDER GIVES YOU ABILITY TO PERSUADE PEOPLE - THE POWER OF PERSUASION.

BAD LUCK GONE

Sometimes things just don't go the way you want. And it's not because you are doing something wrong. Some people say it's bad luck. Just in case this happens to you, prepare the ingredients for this powerful potion in advance!

To make this potion you will need
- DRY CITRUS FRUIT PEEL (ORANGE, LEMON, LIME)
- SUGAR
- PEN AND PAPER
- A BOWL OR GLASS OF WATER

PEEL AN ORANGE (LEMON...) PUT THE PEELS ON A SHEET OF PAPER AND LEAVE THEM IN A SUNNY PLACE OUTSIDE OR IN YOUR HOUSE FOR 3 DAYS (MAYBE EVEN LONGER).

ON A PIECE OF PAPER WRITE 1 WORD FOR EVERY CASE OF BAD LUCK. FOR EXAMPLE, IF YOU LOST SOMETHING, WRITE *LOST*. IF YOU GOT SICK, WRITE *SICK*. IF YOU GOT IN TROUBLE AT SCHOOL WRITE *TROUBLE*. PUT THE PAPER IN A BOWL.

CRUSH THE DRY PEELS (WITH YOUR FINGERS, OR USING MORTAR AND PESTLE), MIX THEM WITH SUGAR AND PUT THIS MIX IN THE BOWL ON TOP OF THE PAPER. NOW POUR WATER INTO THE BOWL, AND SAY THIS SPELL:

BAD LUCK IS IN THE PAST
IT WON'T STAY, IT WON'T LAST.

LEAVE THE BOWL IN THE SUN FOR A FEW HOURS, THEN SPRINKLE THE WATER INSIDE AND AROUND YOUR HOME.

7 Evergreen Keys

This potion locks the doors to secrets you or your friends want to keep safe.

You will need

- LEAVES OR NEEDLES OF ANY EVERGREEN TREE OR BUSH
- SUGAR
- RED THREAD, STRING, OR RIBBON
- PEN AND PAPER
- A BOTTLE OR A JAR

TEAR THE EVERGREEN BRANCH INTO SMALL PIECES. ON PAPER, DRAW CIRCLES IN 2 ROWS, SO THAT **ROW 1 HAS ODD NUMBERS, AND ROW 2 HAS EVEN NUMBERS.** (*EVEN NUMBERS CAN BE DIVIDED INTO 2 EQUAL PARTS. ODD NUMBERS CANNOT*).

PUT EVERGREEN BRANCH PIECES OR NEEDLES INTO EACH CIRCLE. COLLECT THE GREEN PIECES FROM CIRCLES WITH **ODD NUMBERS** AND PUT THEM THEM INTO THE POTION BOTTLE.

SAY: 1, 3, 5 AND 7
          LOCK THE SECRETS OF EARTH AND HEAVEN.

ADD A TEASPOONFUL OF SUGAR, AND FILL THE BOTTLE WITH WATER. IF YOU HAVE LEMON, OR LEMON JUICE, ADD IT TOO, TO MAKE YOUR POTION EVEN STRONGER. NEXT, COLLECT THE GREENS FROM THE CIRCLES WITH EVEN NUMBERS AND DROP THEM INTO THE BOTTLE. TIE THE RED THREAD AROUND THE BOTTLE, SAYING:

2, 4, 6 AND 8
RED SERPENT, GUARD THE GATE!

DIP A FINGER IN THIS POTION AND DRAW THE **EYE OF HORUS,** THE ANCIENT EGYPTIAN SYMBOL OF PROTECTION ON THE WINDOW GLASS IN YOUR ROOM.

THE OLDEST TREE

WHY ARE EVERGREEN TREES LIKE PINE, SPRUCE, AND FIR TREES
SO IMPORTANT FOR MAGIC? WAIT TILL YOU HEAR THIS!
WHAT IS THE OLDEST TREE IN THE WORLD?
HERE IT IS!
NAME: METHUSELAH
KIND: PINE TREE
AGE: 4,850 + YEARS OLD !!!!!
LOCATION: CALIFORNIA, USA
(THE EXACT LOCATION IS SECRET
TO KEEP THIS TREE SAFE!)
SO THIS TREE WAS ALIVE BEFORE
THEY BUILT THE PYRAMIDS IN
ANCIENT EGYPT! ALSO, EVERGREEN
TREES THAT GROW CONES, LIKE
PINE CONES, ARE 200 MILLION YEARS
OLDER THAN THE TREES THAT DROP
LEAVES IN THE FALL. THERE ARE SOME
SCARY OLD TREES IN THE NORTH
LANDING ACADEMY GARDEN...
...AND SCULPTURES
THAT COME ALIVE
AT NIGHT!

THE OGHAM POTION (1)

THIS IS A MIND-READING POTION. IT HELPS YOU UNDERSTAND WHAT A PERSON THINKS, EVEN IF THEY ARE NOT SAYING IT.

THE *OGHAM ALPHABET* (OR TREE ALPHABET) WAS CREATED IN IRELAND AROUND THE 1ST CENTURY A.D. TO WRITE SECRET MESSAGES AND SPELLS. IN THOSE DAYS IN IRELAND THEY WROTE ON STICKS, LOGS, AND TREE BARK USING A KNIFE, SO THEIR LETTERS HAD TO BE EASY TO CUT INTO TREE BARK. ANOTHER REASON WHY THESE LETTERS LOOK LIKE STICKS IS THAT THEY WERE FIRST CREATED AS A **HAND SIGN LANGUAGE.**

EACH LETTER HAS A NAME, AND IT'S A NAME OF A TREE, FOR INSTANCE

B IS BEITH (BIRCH TREE)

D IS DAIR (OAK TREE)

FOR THIS POTION YOU WILL NEED WATER, A FEW TREE BRANCHES, AND YOU WILL NEED TO WRITE YOUR NAME IN THE OGHAM ALPHABET.

A PAGE FROM THE BOOK OF BALLYMOTE WRITTEN IN THE 14TH CENTURY IN IRELAND. IT EXPLAINS THE OGHAM ALPHABET.

THE OGHAM POTION (2)

HERE IS MY NAME IN OGHAM:
WRITE YOUR NAME ON A STRIP
OF PAPER AND USE TAPE OR A PAPER CLIP
TO MAKE IT INTO A BRACELET.
PUT THE BRACELET ON YOUR RIGHT HAND.
BREAK THE BRANCHES INTO SMALL STICKS
AND LEARN TO ASSEMBLE THEM INTO
THE FIRST LETTER OF YOUR NAME.
HERE IS MY LETTER "C"
THEN PLACE YOUR LETTER INSIDE A BOWL.

TOSS IN SOME LEAVES OR FLOWERS,
AND FILL THE BOWL WITH WATER
UNTIL THE BRANCHES AND
LEAVES FLOAT UP. AS YOU
ARE POURING WATER, IMAGINE
THE PERSON WHOSE THOUGHTS
YOU WANT TO KNOW STANDING
UNDER A TREE. SAY THIS SPELL:

FROM THE EARTH, THROUGH THE ROOTS
UP THE BRANCHES I CAME.
EVERY LEAF ON YOUR TREE
SPEAKS MY NAME.
DIP YOUR RIGHT HAND
INTO THE BOWL, AND THEN
TOUCH YOUR FOREHEAD.
SOON THIS PERSON'S
THOUGHTS WILL BECOME
KNOWN TO YOU.

PAPER, BOOK, LIBRARY

WRITING ON TREE BARK? WHATEVER HAPPENED TO PAPER?

PAPER WAS INVENTED IN ANCIENT CHINA BETWEEN 25 AND 220 A.D. BY CAI LUN WHO WORKED AT THE COURT OF THE EMPEROR OF CHINA.

WHAT DID THEY WRITE ON BEFORE PAPER? IN ANCIENT EGYPT THEY WROTE ON SHEETS THEY MADE FROM **PAPYRUS**, A PLANT THAT GROWS ALONG THE RIVER NILE. THE ENGLISH WORD *PAPER* COMES FROM *PAPYRUS*.

BUT IN ANCIENT EUROPE THEY WROTE ON THE BARK OF TREES. OUR WORD *BOOK* COMES FROM ANCIENT GERMAN WORD *BOK* WHICH MEANS **BEECH TREE**!

AND OUR WORD *LIBRARY* COMES FROM THE LATIN WORD *LIBRUM* (= *BOOK*). BEFORE IT CAME TO MEAN *A BOOK*, ITS MEANING WAS... **TREE BARK**!

ANCIENT GREEKS AND ROMANS WROTE ON **PARCHMENT** MADE FROM THE SKIN OF SHEEP OR GOATS, AND ON **TABLETS COVERED WITH BEESWAX** (STUFF BEES USE TO BUILD THEIR HONEYCOMBS). THEY WROTE WITH A FEATHER (**A QUILL**), OR A SHARP STICK THEY CALLED A STYLUS (*STILUS* IN LATIN). OUR WORD **STYLE** COMES FROM **STYLUS**!

THE GREEN BLADE

THIS POTION CLEANS YOUR HOUSE OF ALL BAD ENERGIES.
IT HELPS ALL SADNESS AND ANGER TO GO AWAY.

TO MAKE THIS POTION YOU NEED:
- A TALL GLASS OF WATER
- A GREEN LEAF, A COUPLE
FLOWERS OR BERRIES
- SCISSORS, THREAD, A BEAD
OR SOME SMALL THING YOU CAN
TIE TO A THREAD (A NAIL, A RING)
- A PENCIL

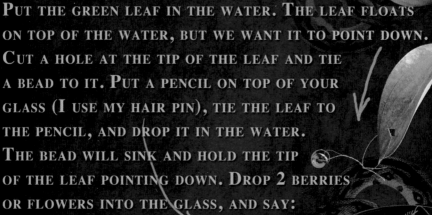

PUT THE GREEN LEAF IN THE WATER. THE LEAF FLOATS
ON TOP OF THE WATER, BUT WE WANT IT TO POINT DOWN.
CUT A HOLE AT THE TIP OF THE LEAF AND TIE
A BEAD TO IT. PUT A PENCIL ON TOP OF YOUR
GLASS (I USE MY HAIR PIN), TIE THE LEAF TO
THE PENCIL, AND DROP IT IN THE WATER.
THE BEAD WILL SINK AND HOLD THE TIP
OF THE LEAF POINTING DOWN. DROP 2 BERRIES
OR FLOWERS INTO THE GLASS, AND SAY:

NIGHT SHADE SNAKE,
MY DOOR IS SHUT.
YOUR EVIL KNOT
MY BLADE WILL CUT.

LEAVE THE GLASS
IN A DARK
PLACE
FOR 1 HOUR, THEN
SPRINKLE THE WATER
AROUND THE HOUSE.

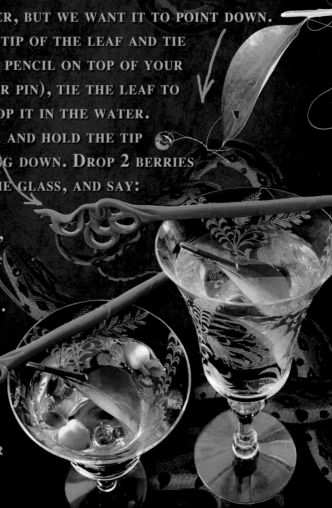

THE ARCHIMEDES PRINCIPLE

When you make potions, you notice that some things float in the water, and others sink. Why?

A ROCK SINKS, AN EGG SINKS, A KEY SINKS, BUT A BRANCH, OR AN APPLE, OR FLOWERS FLOAT ON THE WHATER...
A ROCK IS **HEAVIER THAN WATER,** SO IT PUSHES THE WATER OUT OF THE WAY AND **SINKS,** BUT THE APPLE IS LIGHTER THAN WATER, SO THE WATER PUSHES IT UP AND OUT.

REMEMBER ARCHIMEDES WHO SCREAMED *EUREKA!* WHEN THE WATER SPILLED FROM HIS BATHTUB? HE WAS EXCITED BECAUSE HE HAD DISCOVERED THE **ARCHIMEDES PRINCIPLE! (PRINCIPLE = RULE)**
HIS PRINCIPLE SAYS THAT IF YOU PUT AN OBJECT IN WATER, THE WATER PUSHES IT UP, BUT IF THIS OBJECT IS HEAVIER THAN THE WATER IT CAN REPLACE, IT WILL SINK.
OK, SO WHY DOES A HUGE SHIP FLOAT WHEN IT IS CLEARLY HEAVIER THAN WATER??
WELL, ANY SHIP HAS A LOT OF EMPTY SPACE INSIDE FILLED WITH NOTHING BUT AIR.
AND AIR IS MUCH LIGHTER THAN WATER, SO THE SHIP FLOATS. BUT IF THERE IS A HOLE IN THE SHIP AND THE WATER FILLS ALL THAT EMPTY SPACE, THE SHIP WILL BECOME HEAVIER THAN WATER AND SINK, LIKE THE TITANIC AFTER IT HIT THE ICEBERG!

iceberg
Help!

Charm Potion (1)

This potion will make people like you a lot. It uses the Star River spell.

There is only one kind of magic that makes potions you can drink. It is called **Kitchen Magic, or Kitchen Witchcraft**. The Kitchen Magic potions are not true potions, but enchanted drinks, or even dishes. *Charm Potion* is one of its oldest recipes. Before we start, please read the rules of Kitchen Magic.

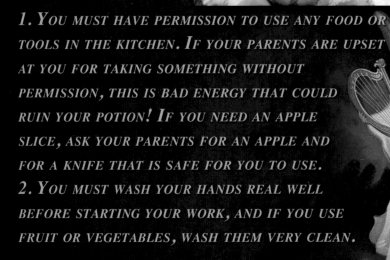

1. You must have permission to use any food or tools in the kitchen. If your parents are upset at you for taking something without permission, this is bad energy that could ruin your potion! If you need an apple slice, ask your parents for an apple and for a knife that is safe for you to use.
2. You must wash your hands real well before starting your work, and if you use fruit or vegetables, wash them very clean.

To make the Charm potion you put slices of fruit or vegetables in a glass of water, cast a spell and leave the potion in a cool place (or refrigerator) for 2 hours. When you drink the potion you cast another spell.
For this potion I use strawberries, cucumber slices, apples, pears, or citrus fruit slices (orange, mandarin, grapefruit, lemon, lime).

Charm Potion (2)

You can make the Charm Potion for yourself, or for friends and family. If you are making it for grownups, remember, they like complex things, so it's good if you use more than 1 ingredient. You can mix

- CUCUMBER AND LEMON
- ORANGE AND STRAWBERRY
- STRAWBERRY AND CUCUMBER

Or, add herbs or spices if you have them in your family's kitchen. Add

- BASIL TO CUCUMBER
- MINT TO CUCUMBER, LEMON, STRAWBERRY
- CINNAMON TO APPLE, ORANGE
- CLOVES TO ORANGES
- ROSEMARY TO GRAPEFRUIT

You can also add ice and offer it with a straw. Use only drinking water (ask your parents which water is safe in your area - tap, filtered, or bottled). And now, on to the spells!

CUCUMBER AND LIME
STRAWBERRY AND LEMON

CINNAMON   *MINT*
  CLOVES   *BASIL*

Charm Potion (3)

Use these spells to fill your potion with magic power.

"Starry Night" by Dutch painter Van Gogh

If 10 and 9 will make 19,
If 8 and 7 make 15,
If 6 and 5 will make 11,
If 4 and 3 together 7,
If 2 and 1 together 3,
Star River, come to me.

Drinking the potion, say:
Star River, give me a star!
My light will shine
Near and far.

What is cinnamon? It's the bark of the cinnamon tree, which comes from the island of Sri Lanka (its old name is Ceylon). In ancient Rome cinnamon was 15 times more expensive than silver, and in the Middle Ages doctors used it to treat cold and flu. You can try it: Put a spoonful of honey and a stick of cinnamon (or a pinch of ground cinnamon) into a cup of warm milk. Drink it yourself, or make it for your family if someone catches a cold.

What are cloves? Cloves are dried flower buds coming from Indonesia. Long ago in Indonesia they planted a clove tree for every child born and believed the lives of the child and the tree were magically linked.

THE SNAKE OF ASGARD

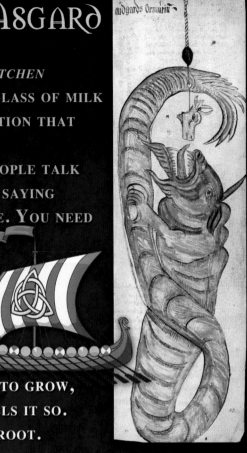

Midgards Ormurinn

HERE IS AN ANCIENT VIKING *KITCHEN MAGIC* SPELL YOU SAY OVER A GLASS OF MILK IN ORDER TO TURN IT INTO A POTION THAT PROTECTS YOU FROM GOSSIP.

WHAT IS GOSSIP? IT'S WHEN PEOPLE TALK ABOUT YOU BEHIND YOUR BACK, SAYING THINGS THAT ARE OFTEN UNTRUE. YOU NEED

• A GLASS OF MILK
• A BLACK STONE

HOLD YOUR MAGIC WAND OVER THE GLASS, AND SAY:

THE EVIL GRASS DOESN'T HAVE TO GROW,
BUT THE SNAKE OF ASGARD TELLS IT SO.
MY WORD WILL CUT IT AT THE ROOT.
MY TRUTH WILL CRUSH ITS EVIL FRUIT.

TAKE THE BLACK STONE IN YOUR HAND, AND SAY THESE WORDS BEFORE DRINKING THE MILK:

MOONLIGHT, TOUCH THIS STONE
AND MAKE MY TRUTH BE KNOWN.

WORLD SERPENT

THOR'S HAMMER

THE SNAKE OF ASGARD IS THE MIDGARD SERPENT (OR WORLD SERPENT). VIKINGS BELIEVED THAT IT WRAPS AROUND THE WORLD, HOLDING ITS TAIL IN ITS MOUTH (LIKE *OUROBOROUS* - READ ABOUT IT IN MY BOOK *STAR MAGIC*), AND THAT ONE TIME THOR, THE GOD OF THUNDER, CAUGHT THE SERPENT WHEN FISHING. SEE THE SERPENT AND THE FISHING HOOK WITH A COW HEAD ON IT IN THE PICTURE ABOVE.

The Sunlit Heart Potion

One more kitchen magic recipe. This potion will give joy of life to your family if mixed into their food.

You'll need to ask grownups for some ingredients. Tell them you will make **an infused oil** for them to use in cooking. Your method is **cold infusion with fresh ingredients.** You need to say these words, so they understand that you know what you are doing! You will need

- SOME OLIVE OIL
- A JAR WITH A LID
- ANY OF THESE FRESH INGREDIENTS:

PARSLEY, MINT, BASIL, DILL, ROSEMARY, OREGANO, BAY LEAF

Tell your family they can choose their flavor!!!

- PEN, PAPER AND THREAD OR RIBBON.

First, wash your hands well. Next, wash the herbs. Tear the leaves and stems into small pieces, mash them with a fork or mortar and pestle and put them in the jar. Pour the olive oil on top until the herb is covered. Now think of the names of every person in your family with whom you want to share the magic of joy. Take the third letter from every person's name and write it on a small strip of paper. For example, my son is Eric, and his dad is Scott, so I write: I. O.

Say this spell:

The power of my magic art

Will put sunlight in your heart.

Attach it with a thread to the jar,

close the lid and

give it to your family.

Ask them to use it within 3 days.

Magic Flower Water

This is an elixir. Its magic power depends on the color of the flowers you use.

The Flower Water elixir uses press-dried flowers. This process of drying flowers takes 7 to 10 days. Make sure your flowers don't have any water drops on them. Put them face down on a sheet of paper, cover with another sheet, and put a few heavy books on top. The books will press the flowers flat. Wait for 7 days, and check if the flowers are dry.

To make the elixir, put a few dry flowers into a glass or a jar, press them with a clean rock or shell, and cover them with water. Use this chart to choose what color flowers to dry for your elixir.

FLOWER COLOR	MAGIC POWER OF THE ELIXIR
RED	DESTROYS FEAR
ORANGE OR YELLOW	REVEALS SECRETS IN YOUR DREAMS
BLUE OR PURPLE	GIVES YOU POWER TO SEE THINGS INVISIBLE TO OTHERS
GREEN	MAKES PEOPLE LISTEN TO YOU

Sprinkle this potion on the clothes you wear every morning for 3 days, saying this spell:

Wisdom of the earth, sleeping in this flower
Wake up and bloom again as my own power.

A Witch's Bottle

Is anyone trying to put a spell on you?
Defend yourself with this ancient potion.

To make this potion you will need:

- A spoonful of dirt from outside
- A bottle of water
- A leaf of a plant (or a paper leaf)
- A feather (or a paper feather)
- Pen or marker

Use a table spoon to dig some dirt outside,
making sure not to touch it with your hands.
Mix a spoonful of this dirt in some water
and fill a bottle with this mixture.
Use a marker to write NO on the
leaf and on the feather.
Writing on a feather is hard.
A paper feather is fine.
Hold the leaf above the bottle,
and speak these magic words:

> Whether I know you, or do not know,
> Your evil magic will not grow.

Drop the leaf into the bottle, and hold
the feather above the bottle, saying:
Near or far, low or high
Your evil magic now will die.
Drop the feather into the bottle.
Shake it well, then take it outside, and
pour everything out under a tree.

ARE LOVE POTIONS REAL?

HA-HA-HA-HA!!! THAT'S HOW I RESPOND WHEN MY STUDENTS ASK ME THIS QUESTION!

YES, SOME PEOPLE BELIEVE THAT IF THEY MIX UP A SILLY DRINK AND SPRINKLE IT WITH ROSE PETALS, THE PERSON WHO DRINKS IT WILL FALL IN LOVE WITH THEM.

ONCE I AM DONE LAUGHING AT THIS IN MY POTIONS CLASS AT THE NORTH LANDING ACADEMY OF MAGIC ARTS, I TELL MY STUDENTS: IF ANYONE SAYS THEY CAN MAKE A LOVE POTION, THIS PERSON IS A **CHARLATAN!** A *CHARLATAN* (SHAR-LA-TAN) IS A PERSON WHO PRETENDS THEY HAVE A SKILL OR KNOWLEDGE IN ORDER TO DECEIVE OTHERS.

REMEMBER ONCE AND FOR ALL: YOUR HEART HAS DIVINE LIGHT IN IT. THIS LIGHT IS A MAGIC SHIELD. IT PROTECTS YOU FROM ANYONE TRYING TO MESS WITH THE GREATEST TREASURE YOU KEEP THERE - LOVE.

OK, THEN MY STUDENTS ASK ME: IF LOVE POTIONS ARE NOT REAL, HOW CAN I MAKE A PERSON FALL IN LOVE WITH ME? HERE IS WHAT I TELL THEM: BECOME THE BEST YOU CAN BE, SO PEOPLE FALL IN LOVE WITH YOU WITHOUT ANY POTIONS! GROW YOUR TALENTS, LEARN A LOT OF SKILLS, FEAR NOTHING, NEVER GIVE UP. IF YOU ARE AWESOME (AND I KNOW YOU WILL BE, IF YOU ARE BRAVE ENOUGH TO STUDY MAGIC) IT WILL BE EASY TO FALL IN LOVE WITH YOU! I WOULD!

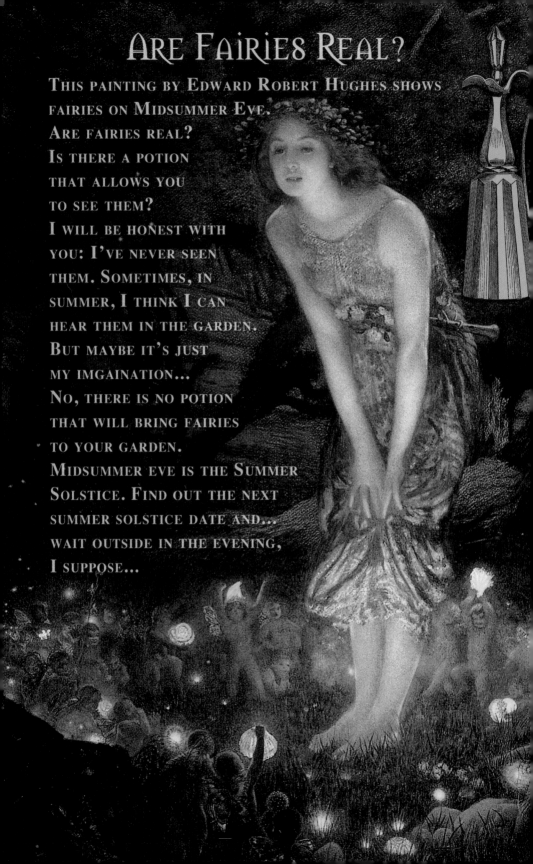

ARE FAIRIES REAL?

THIS PAINTING BY EDWARD ROBERT HUGHES SHOWS FAIRIES ON MIDSUMMER EVE. ARE FAIRIES REAL? IS THERE A POTION THAT ALLOWS YOU TO SEE THEM? I WILL BE HONEST WITH YOU: I'VE NEVER SEEN THEM. SOMETIMES, IN SUMMER, I THINK I CAN HEAR THEM IN THE GARDEN. BUT MAYBE IT'S JUST MY IMGAINATION... NO, THERE IS NO POTION THAT WILL BRING FAIRIES TO YOUR GARDEN. MIDSUMMER EVE IS THE SUMMER SOLSTICE. FIND OUT THE NEXT SUMMER SOLSTICE DATE AND... WAIT OUTSIDE IN THE EVENING, I SUPPOSE...

Word of Warning

One last thing. Whenever you are working on a potion, the magic energy around you is so strong, dragons can feel it from far away... Keep your wand at hand, and practice the Horizon Circle. Sometimes dragons are invisible until really close. But you will know.

Stay safe.
Much love to you.

Made in the USA
Columbia, SC
08 January 2021

30543692R00020